Two Tough Crocs

by DAVID BEDFORD

Illustrated by TOM JELLETT

Holiday House / New York

Text copyright © 2013 by David Bedford
Illustrations copyright © 2013 by Tom Jellett

First published in Australia in 2013 as *Sylvester & Arnold* by Little Hare Books (an imprint of Hardie Grant Egmont).
First published in the United States of America in 2014 by Holiday House, New York.

Library of Congress Cataloging-in-Publication Data
Bedford, David, 1969-
[Sylvester and Arnold]
Two tough crocs / by David Bedford ; illustrated by Tom Jellett. — First edition.
pages cm
"First published in Australia in 2013 as *Sylvester & Arnold* by Little Hare Books (an imprint of Hardie Grant Egmont)."
Summary: Sylvester and Arnold enjoy being big, tough crocodiles so when
they finally meet they are about to fight until Betty,
an enormous crocodile, comes hissing by to take
over their swamp.
ISBN 978-0-8234-3048-2 (hardcover)
[1. Crocodiles—Fiction. 2. Friendship—Fiction.]
I. Jellett, Tom, illustrator. II. Title.
PZ7.B3817995Two 2014
[E]—dc23
2013023666

Sylvester was a
big, tough croc.

So was Arnold.

Sylvester wore tough-croc shorts,
a tough-croc vest, and tough-croc boots.
When he went out to play, he put on
an ugly, tough-croc face.

So did Arnold.

Sylvester spent all day making sure everyone knew how tough he was.

He snapped branches in his jaws and chased small animals for fun.

So did Arnold.

The swamp was big and wide,
and Sylvester and Arnold had never met.

Until one day...

they **bumped** into each other.

Sylvester **bared his teeth**. So did Arnold.

Sylvester made his **eyes look bulgy**. So did Arnold.

Sylvester grabbed Arnold with his **favorite two-claw grip.**

He got ready to throw Arnold over his shoulder.

Arnold grabbed Sylvester with *his* **favorite two-claw grip.**

He got ready to knock Sylvester sideways with a swipe of his tail.

But suddenly they heard a loud **hiss.** . . .

It was an **ENORMOUS** croc.

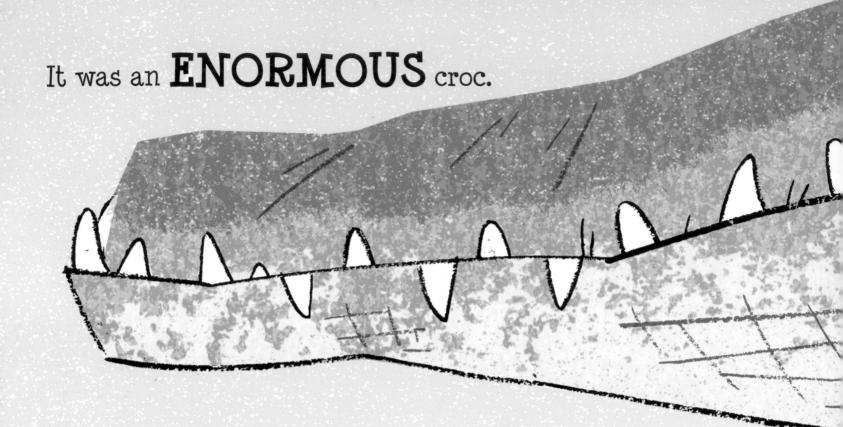

She had the **ugliest** tough-croc face
and **bulgiest** tough-croc eyes
Sylvester and Arnold had ever seen.

"I'm called Betty,"
she roared. "Betty the Bad!
I'm moving into this swamp!
And I'm so big and tough,
no one can stop me!"

Betty grabbed Sylvester and Arnold in a
GIGANTIC two-claw grip.

Then . . .

Sylvester and Arnold landed
in the deepest, slimiest,
boggiest hole in the swamp.

They watched Betty the Bad snapping whole trees, chasing away the other animals, and messing up their toys. **"This is my swamp now,"** she bellowed.

Sylvester and Arnold didn't feel like big, tough crocs anymore.

"I'm going to find a new swamp to live in," said Sylvester.

"So am I," said Arnold.

Sylvester and Arnold didn't dare to move until it was dark.

"I'm scared that Betty will see us," said Sylvester.

"So am I," said Arnold.

Sylvester held Arnold with his favorite
two-claw grip to help him feel safer.

Arnold held Sylvester with his favorite
two-claw grip to help him feel braver.

Then they set off
to find new swamps.

Betty watched something creeping from the **slimiest, boggiest** hole in the swamp.

"Whatever that is, I'm going to scare it away," she said.

But when she tiptoed closer, she saw . . .

two shaking heads with **rattling teeth** . . .

four staring eyes . . . eight gripping claws . .

and **two hard, knobbly tails.**

It was the **scariest** thing Betty had ever seen.

"Help!"
Betty cried.

She ran one way . . .

then the other way . . .

then around in circles . . .

and fell straight into
the deepest, slimiest,
boggiest hole in the swamp.

Betty didn't look like a
big, tough croc anymore.

Sylvester looked at Arnold.

Arnold looked at Sylvester.

Then they reached out with their two-claw grips
and helped Betty climb out of the boggy hole.

After that...

Sylvester was **still** a **big, tough croc**.

He wore tough-croc shorts,
a tough-croc vest, and tough-croc boots.

But when he went out to play, he always had a
happy, friendly croc face.

So did his new **best friends**,
Betty and Arnold.